# FLIGHT

*written by* Fiona Campbell
*illustrated by* Studio Boni/Galante,
Ivan Stalio *and* Lorenzo Cecchi

**Ladybird**

# CONTENTS

# INTRODUCTION

There are lots of stories in history about people trying to fly like birds. Some people tried to fly using huge wings attached to their arms. Other people used over-sized cloaks, like parachutes, or built incredible flapping machines, but still they could not fly.

An early attempt to fly.

**Successful flying**
We can now travel faster, higher and further than any bird or insect.

The first real plane flew less than one hundred years ago. But, since then, there have been incredible advances in flight technology. People have even travelled to the Moon.

5

# HOT-AIR BALLOONS

In 1783, a sheep, a cockerel and a duck were the first living things to fly in a machine. They were not in a plane, but in a hot-air balloon. It was built by the Montgolfier brothers. A few weeks later, a person made the first balloon flight.

**Ballooning**
The first hot-air balloon flight was made in a balloon called the *Montgolfière*.

A hot-air balloon rises as air inside it is heated by burners. The hot air is lighter than the cooler air outside, and as hot air rises, so the balloon floats up. The balloon floats down when the air cools. Burners are used in flight to heat the air in the balloon, to keep the balloon up. To land, the pilot opens a **vent** and the hot air escapes.

**Controlling height**

Bags of sand, kept in the passenger compartment, hold the balloon down before lift-off.

The pilot can make the balloon rise even higher by throwing out some of the bags of sand.

# AIRSHIPS

If you wanted to cross the Atlantic Ocean by air in 1930, you would have travelled in an airship. The journey took about two days. Airships were like huge bags of gas. The larger airships had rigid metal frames which were covered by cloth. Each airship had chambers filled with **hydrogen**, which made the airship lighter than air.

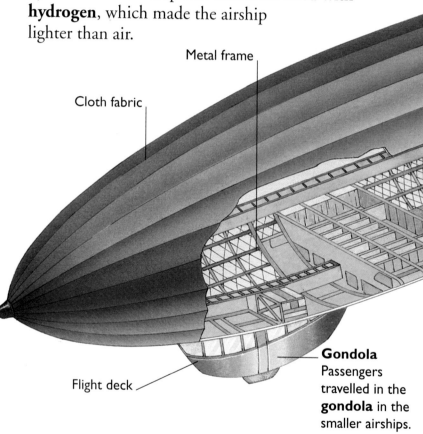

Metal frame

Cloth fabric

Flight deck

**Gondola**
Passengers travelled in the **gondola** in the smaller airships.

**Dangers of airship travel**

In 1929, an airship called the *Graf Zeppelin* flew around the world. But a series of disasters, caused by explosive hydrogen gas, brought airship travel to an end. Modern airships are smaller than those built in the 1930s, and filled with non-explosive helium gas.

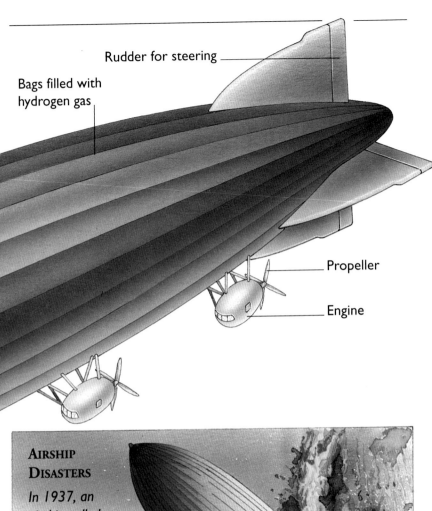

Rudder for steering

Bags filled with
hydrogen gas

Propeller

Engine

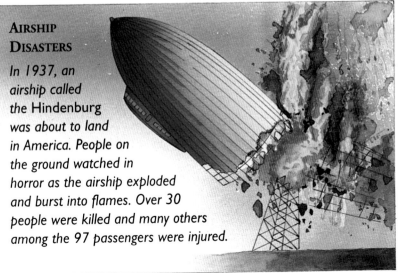

**AIRSHIP DISASTERS**

*In 1937, an airship called the Hindenburg was about to land in America. People on the ground watched in horror as the airship exploded and burst into flames. Over 30 people were killed and many others among the 97 passengers were injured.*

# THE SECRETS OF FLIGHT

Birds and planes can fly. But they are heavier than air, so how do they fly? To stay in the air, a bird and a plane need a push upwards to balance their weight. This is called **lift** and it is made by wings. The air slows down anything that moves through it. This is **drag**. To keep moving, a plane or bird needs a push, called **thrust**, to overcome the drag.

## Lift

Air rushes over the top of the wing faster than it travels underneath. This lifts a bird or plane into the air.

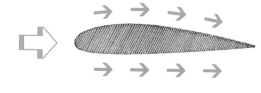

## Shaped like a frisbee

Wings are curved on top and flatter underneath. This shape is called an **aerofoil** and it is essential to winged flight. A frisbee is like a flying wing. It flies through the air because its top surface is curved, in the same way as the top of a wing. Spinning the frisbee helps keep it level.

## Drag

When a bird flies, the force of the air tries to slow the bird down. It is the same force that you feel when you run and feel the air pushing against your face.

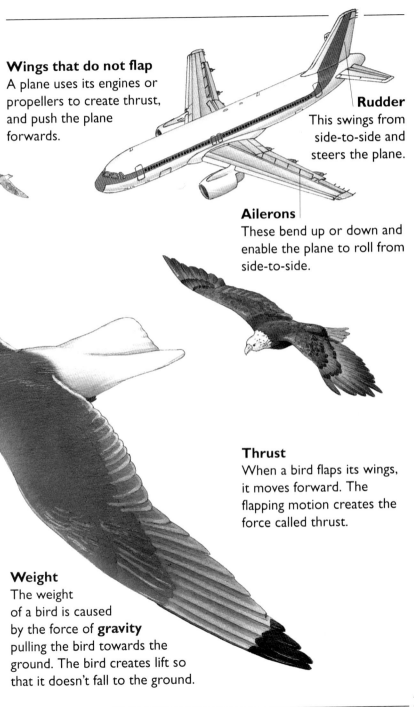

**Wings that do not flap**
A plane uses its engines or propellers to create thrust, and push the plane forwards.

**Rudder**
This swings from side-to-side and steers the plane.

**Ailerons**
These bend up or down and enable the plane to roll from side-to-side.

**Thrust**
When a bird flaps its wings, it moves forward. The flapping motion creates the force called thrust.

**Weight**
The weight of a bird is caused by the force of **gravity** pulling the bird towards the ground. The bird creates lift so that it doesn't fall to the ground.

11

# GLIDERS

Gliders are planes with no engines to power them. To take off, gliders are towed by a plane or truck. The glider rises into the air and the tow cable is released. Gliders use rising currents of hot air, called **thermals**, to fly.

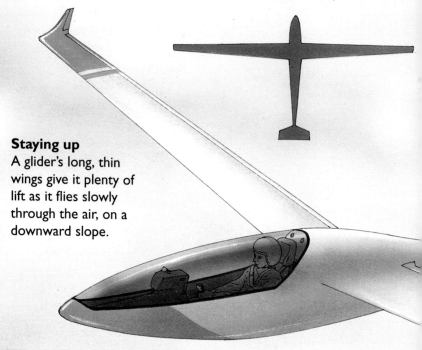

**Staying up**
A glider's long, thin wings give it plenty of lift as it flies slowly through the air, on a downward slope.

CAYLEY'S GLIDER
*Sir George Cayley experimented with different shapes of gliders. His best design was a **triplane**. It had three sets of wings, made from strong cloth stretched over a wooden frame. A frightened ten-year old boy made the first flight in Cayley's glider in 1849.*

# HANG-GLIDING

Hang-gliders use air currents just like a bird. The wings of a hang-glider are light and the pilot is suspended by a harness and a trapeze-like bar. The pilot takes off from a steep hill or mountain top.

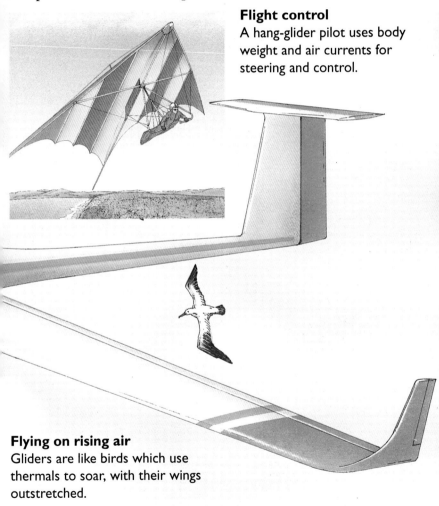

### Flight control
A hang-glider pilot uses body weight and air currents for steering and control.

**Flying on rising air**
Gliders are like birds which use thermals to soar, with their wings outstretched.

# POWERED FLIGHT

People built gliders to test their theories about flight. Early aviators realised that an engine was needed to build a useful plane that could travel long distances. Rather than using a heavy steam engine for power, two American brothers, called Orville and Wilbur Wright, had the idea of using a home-built lightweight petrol engine.

*Flyer I*
An early kind of powered
**biplane**, with two sets of wings.

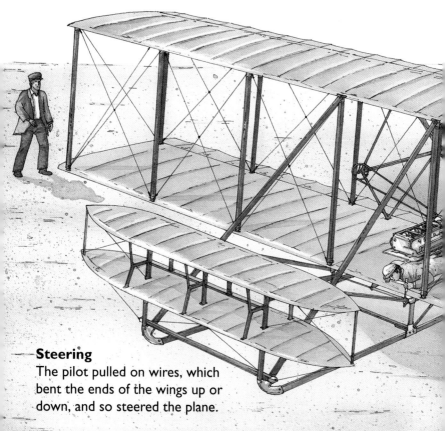

**Steering**
The pilot pulled on wires, which bent the ends of the wings up or down, and so steered the plane.

In 1903, the Wright Brothers built a plane called *Flyer I*. Wilbur tried to fly it, but the plane crashed before taking off. Two days later, with Orville as pilot, they tried again. This time, *Flyer I* took off and travelled 37 metres. It only stayed in the air for about twelve seconds, but *Flyer I* had made the first powered flight in history.

# EARLY FLIGHT
# RECORD BREAKERS

| PILOT | LANDMARK | DATE | FLIGHT REPORT |
|---|---|---|---|
| Bartolomeu de Gusmão (Brazil) | Earliest recorded unmanned hot-air balloon flight | 1709 | The balloon was flown indoors |
| Henri Giffard (France) | Earliest flight in an airship | 1852 | The airship was powered by a steam engine |
| Otto Lilienthal (Germany) | Made controlled flights in a hang-glider | 1894 | Flights as far as 350 metres |
| Wilbur Wright (America) | First flight over 5 minutes | 1904 | *Flyer II* travelled over 4 kilometres |
| Paul Cornu (France) | The first flight in a helicopter | 1907 | Lifted only half a metre in the air |
| Louis Blériot (France) | First person to fly across the English Channel | 1909 | The flight took 36 minutes |
| Charles Lindbergh (America) | First nonstop solo flight across the Atlantic | 1927 | The flight took 33 hours and 29 minutes |
| Amy Johnson (Britain) | First woman to fly solo from Britain to Australia | 1930 | The journey lasted 20 days |
| Wiley Post (America) | First solo flight around the world | 1933 | The journey took 8 days |

Navigation display

Engine display

Flight display

Engine throttles

Pilot

# A JUMBO JET

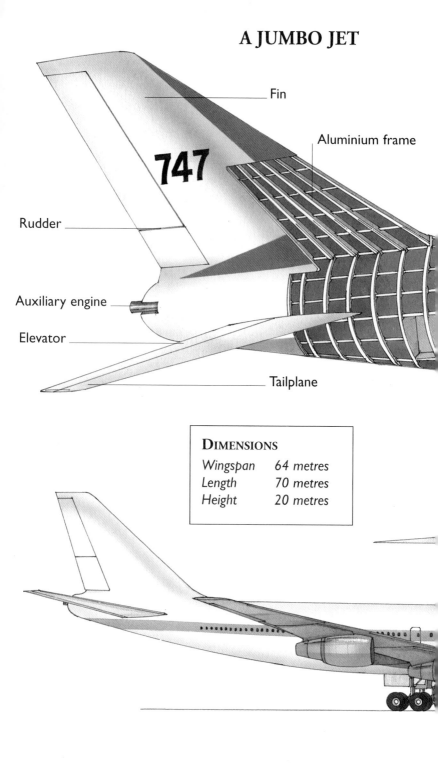

Fin

Aluminium frame

Rudder

Auxiliary engine

Elevator

Tailplane

**DIMENSIONS**

*Wingspan*    64 *metres*
*Length*      70 *metres*
*Height*      20 *metres*

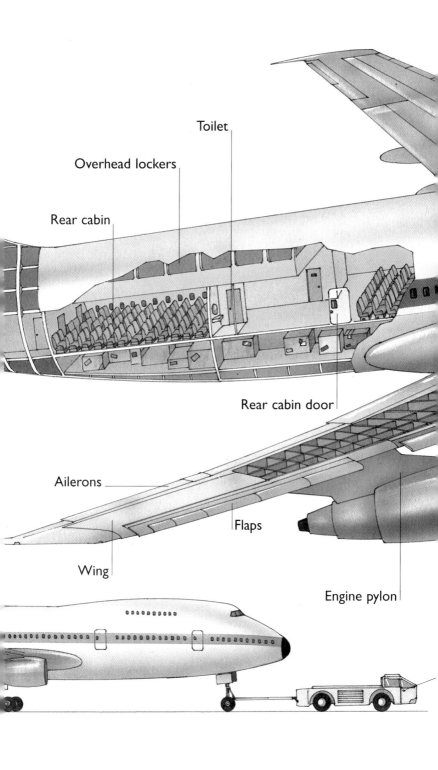

Toilet

Overhead lockers

Rear cabin

Rear cabin door

Ailerons

Flaps

Wing

Engine pylon

# THE AIRPORT

Outside the terminal building aircraft are serviced before their next flight. This involves cleaning, refuelling and restocking. When the passengers and their baggage are on board, the aircraft is ready for take-off.

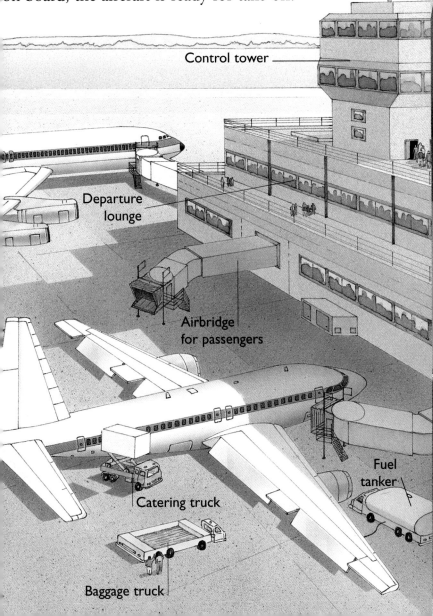

Control tower

Departure lounge

Airbridge for passengers

Catering truck

Fuel tanker

Baggage truck

Overhead control panel

Control column

Brakes

Co-pilot

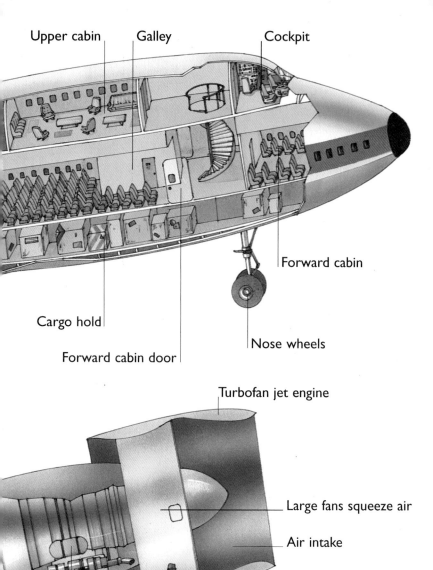

Upper cabin   Galley   Cockpit

Forward cabin

Cargo hold

Forward cabin door

Nose wheels

Turbofan jet engine

Large fans squeeze air

Air intake

Maintenance engineer

Fuel burns here

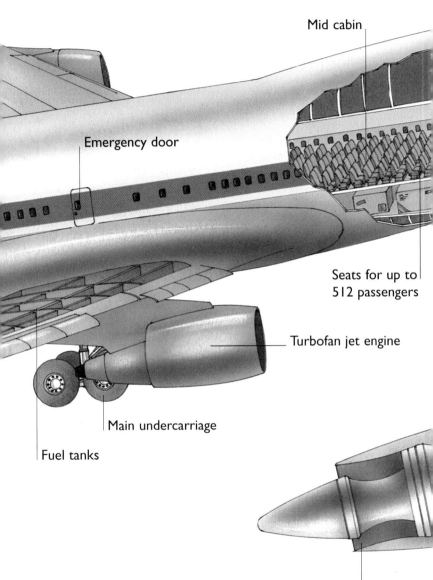

Mid cabin

Emergency door

Seats for up to
512 passengers

Turbofan jet engine

Main undercarriage

Fuel tanks

Aircraft towing truck
moves aircraft on ground
when engines are off.

Stream of hot gas shoots out,
pushing aircraft along.

# AIR TRAFFIC CONTROL

The pilot can only **taxi** to the runway and take off when he has permission from the control tower. Once airborne, an air traffic controller tells the pilot which direction to fly in.

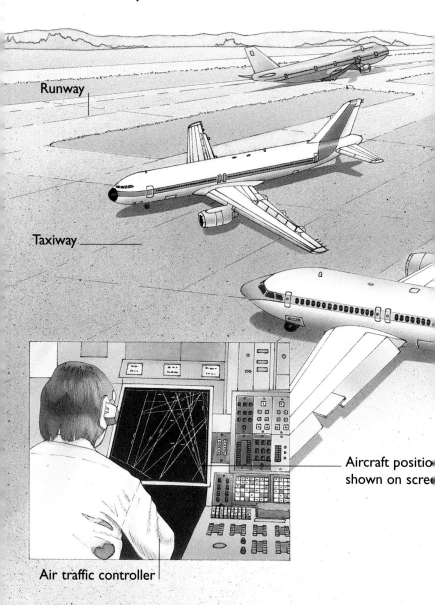

Runway

Taxiway

Aircraft position shown on screen

Air traffic controller

# FLYING BOATS

Flying boats, or seaplanes, are planes which take off and land on water. During the 1930s they were used to carry passengers and mail. Nowadays they are used mainly for transport in remote areas and fighting large fires. They scoop up water as they fly over the sea or a lake and drop water on the fire.

## A seaplane

Some seaplanes have floats where normal planes have wheels.

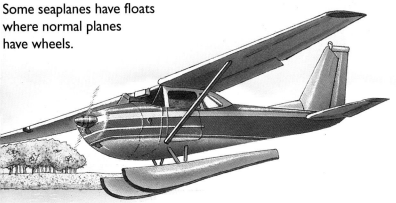

### Seaplane landing

The body of a seaplane is like the hull of a boat. Floats on the wings keep the seaplane steady as it lands on water.

# JETS

In 1937 a new source of power that would completely change the world of flight was first tested. This was the jet engine. Jet engines allow modern planes to fly fast and far. The jet engine works by sucking in air at one end and forcing compressed air out, at great speed, at the other end. This thrusts the plane forward.

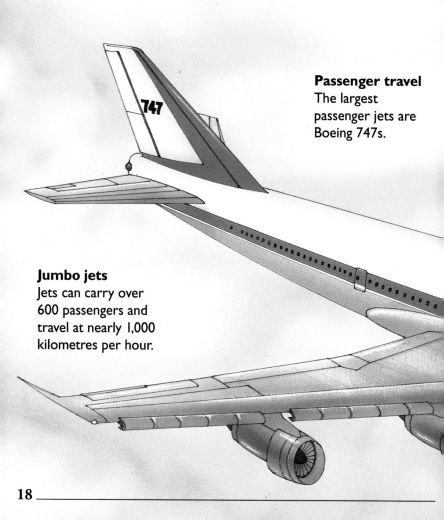

**Passenger travel**
The largest passenger jets are Boeing 747s.

**Jumbo jets**
Jets can carry over 600 passengers and travel at nearly 1,000 kilometres per hour.

# CONCORDE

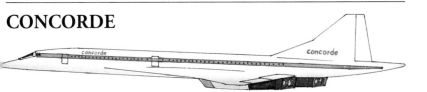

*Concorde* carries 128 passengers and travels faster than the speed of sound (1,124 kilometres per hour). The journey from Paris to New York only takes just over three hours.

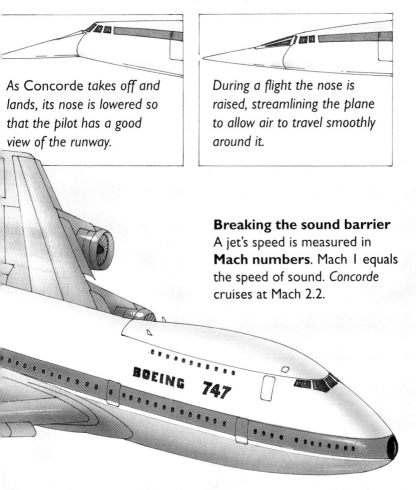

As Concorde *takes off and lands, its nose is lowered so that the pilot has a good view of the runway.*

*During a flight the nose is raised, streamlining the plane to allow air to travel smoothly around it.*

**Breaking the sound barrier**
A jet's speed is measured in **Mach numbers**. Mach 1 equals the speed of sound. *Concorde* cruises at Mach 2.2.

BOEING 747

# HELICOPTERS

Helicopters are very useful because they can land and take off vertically. They are used for many special jobs, such as rescues in dangerous places and as ambulances. They also carry supplies, crew and equipment to oil rigs.

## Manoeuvrability

The main rotor blades are like bird's wings – they spin round and so provide lift. The rotor blades also make the helicopter fly up and down, forwards and backwards and side-to-side.

## The rotors

These are the horizontal blades. When they are kept level and rotate fast, the helicopter hovers.

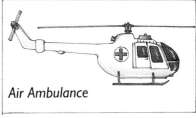

*Air Ambulance*

*Military Operations*

## The tail rotor

This stops the body of the helicopter from spinning round and is used to steer the helicopter left or right.

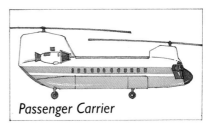

*Passenger Carrier*

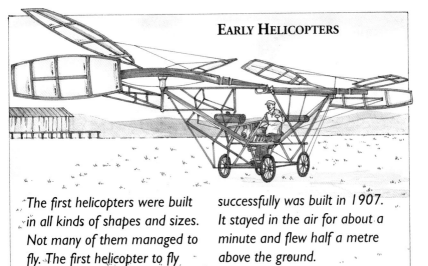

### EARLY HELICOPTERS

*The first helicopters were built in all kinds of shapes and sizes. Not many of them managed to fly. The first helicopter to fly successfully was built in 1907. It stayed in the air for about a minute and flew half a metre above the ground.*

# SPACE TRAVEL

When a rocket is launched, fuel burns and produces gases. These gases blast out with a huge force, overcoming the Earth's gravity and so the rocket flies into space.

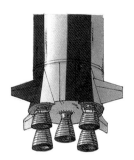

**Several engines**
Each stage of a rocket has its own engines.

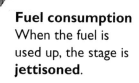

**Fuel consumption**
When the fuel is used up, the stage is **jettisoned**.

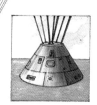

### BACK TO EARTH

*The crew return to Earth in the command module, which splashes into the sea.*

During the 1950s and 1960s, there was a 'space race' between Russia and America. The first person to travel into space was Russian astronaut, Yuri Gagarin in 1961. But the first person to walk on the Moon was American astronaut, Neil Armstrong, on 20 July 1969.

**Saturn V**
The world's largest space rocket, 110 metres tall.

**Eternal imprint**
Neil Armstrong's footprints are still imprinted in the dust on the Moon. There is never any wind there to blow them away.

# SPACE SHUTTLES

Unlike rockets, which can only be used once, a space shuttle can be used for several missions. A control centre on the ground launches and controls the shuttle during its mission, which usually lasts for several days. The plane-like part of the shuttle is called the **orbiter**.

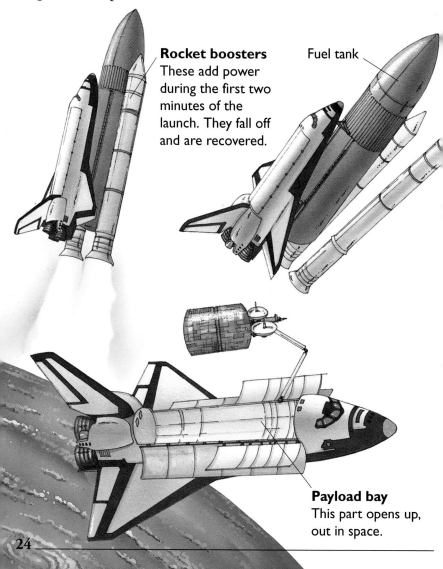

**Rocket boosters**
These add power during the first two minutes of the launch. They fall off and are recovered.

Fuel tank

**Payload bay**
This part opens up, out in space.

Space shuttles carry satellites and telescopes into space in their **payload** bay. Astronauts sometimes carry out experiments in a laboratory on board. Astronauts venture outside the shuttle to repair broken satellites.

**In the vacuum of space**
Outside the shuttle, astronauts wear a backpack which propels them through space.

Hand controls

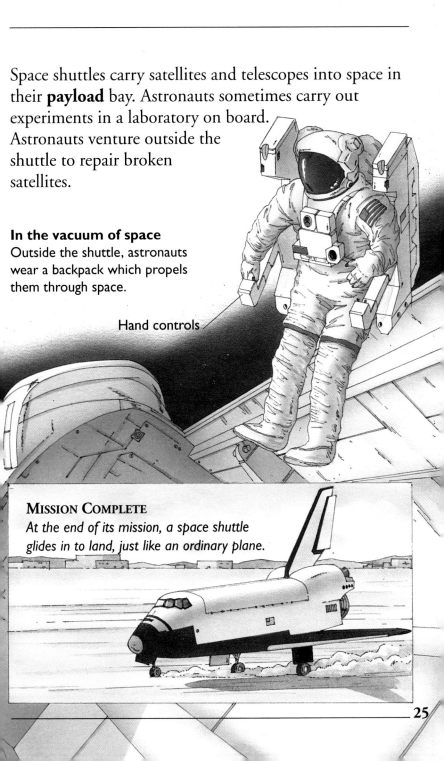

MISSION COMPLETE
*At the end of its mission, a space shuttle glides in to land, just like an ordinary plane.*

25

# FLYING CREATURES

Birds are not the only creatures that can fly. Some insects, such as bees and dragonflies, can perform manoeuvres that make birds look clumsy by comparison.

### Flying insects
Wasps and bees beat their wings up and down about 200 times a second. Insects can dart, twist and turn in the air with ease.

### Dragonflies
Dragonflies hover like helicopters when they feed. Their wings flap fifty times a second. The fast beating of wings creates the familiar buzzing sound.

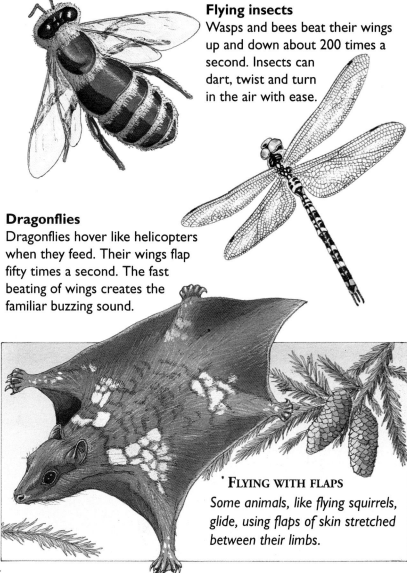

### FLYING WITH FLAPS
Some animals, like flying squirrels, glide, using flaps of skin stretched between their limbs.

### Hawks glide
Like glider planes, birds such as eagles and hawks glide without moving their wings. They soar on thermals or air rising up cliffs.

### Fruit bats
Apart from birds and insects, the only other animals that fly by flapping their wings are bats.

CAN FISH FLY?
*Flying fish do not really fly, but glide. They build up speed while swimming, then take off from the surface of the water, and fall back in again.*

# AMAZING FLIGHT FACTS

- **The fast falcon**  The fastest flying creature is the peregrine falcon. It can fly at 270 kilometres per hour when swooping to catch its prey.

- **Paper plane**  The longest indoor flight by a paper plane, launched by hand, is 59 metres.

- **Round the world**  In 1986, two pilots flew around the world without stopping for fuel. They travelled a total of 40,212 kilometres in nine days in a plane called *Voyager*.

- **The albatross**  The wandering albatross has the largest wingspan of any bird. The wings measure about three metres from tip-to-tip when outstretched.

- **High flyers**  Two hot-air balloons, *Star Flyer 1* and *Star Flyer 2*, flew over the top of Mount Everest in 1991.

- **The first helicopter**  The first person to have the idea of the helicopter was the Italian artist Leonardo da Vinci, who lived from 1452 to 1519.

- **Blind as a bat**  Bats can fly in the dark by making sounds which echo back to tell the bat where it is. Even blind bats can fly.

- **Long distance butterflies**  Butterflies can fly far. Some fly across continents and oceans but they can settle on land or sea, to rest.

# GLOSSARY

**Aerofoil** The special shape of a wing. It causes air to flow faster over the top of the wing than the bottom. This creates lift.

**Biplane** A plane with two pairs of wings, one above the other.

**Drag** A force which slows down an object moving through the air. It occurs because the object has to push air out of the way as it moves.

**Gondola** A cabin which hangs underneath an airship. The flight deck of an airship is usually inside its gondola.

**Gravity** The force which pulls every object towards the centre of the Earth. Gravity is the weight that an object or an animal has.

**Hydrogen** A gas which weighs less than air. Hydrogen was used to fill airships to make them rise up into the air.

**Jettison** To throw out equipment or cargo in order to lighten the vessel.

**Lift** The upward pull caused by wings. It keeps a plane or a bird in the air. Lift is made when air flows over and under a wing.

**Mach number** A way of measuring the speed of a plane. Mach 1 is equal to the speed of sound (1,124 kilometres per hour). A plane which can fly faster than Mach 1 is supersonic.

**Orbiter** A space shuttle which travels in a circle around the Moon, or a planet, but does not land on the surface.

**Payload** A satellite or another object that a spacecraft carries into space.

**Taxi** When an aircraft moves slowly along the ground, before take-off and after landing.

**Thermal** A rising current of warm air. Thermals occur when air is heated by the warm ground beneath.

**Thrust** The push which keeps a plane or bird moving through the air. Thrust is needed because drag slows a plane or bird down.

**Triplane** A plane with three pairs of wings. The pairs of wings lie one above the other.

**Vent** A hole which air or gases can go through. A vent can be opened or closed.

# INDEX *(Entries in **bold** refer to an illustration)*